SHIBUMI
AND THE KITEMAKER

渋味

Text and illustrations copyright © 1999 by Mercer Mayer
Marshall Cavendish, 99 White Plains Road, Tarrytown, NY 10591

Library of Congress Cataloging-in-Publication Data
Mayer, Mercer, date
Shibumi and the kitemaker / by Mercer Mayer.
p. cm.
Summary: After seeing the disparity between the conditions of her father's palace and the city beyond
its walls, the emperor's daughter has the royal kitemaker build a huge kite to take her away from it all.
ISBN 0-7614-5145-5
[1. Fathers and daughters—Fiction. 2. Japan—Fiction. 3. Kites—Fiction.] I. Title
PZ7.M462Sh   1999   [E]—dc21   98-49700 CIP   AC

The text of the book is set in 16 point Hiroshige Book.
The illustrations were created in Adobe Photoshop, ElectricImage, FormZ, Bryce, Painter,
Adobe Illustrator, and Tree Professional.
Printed in Italy
First Marshall Cavendish Paperbacks Editions 2003

6 5 4 3 2 1

SHIBUMI
AND THE KITEMAKER

STORY AND PICTURES BY MERCER MAYER

Marshall Cavendish New York

For Gina, my loving wife

SHIBUMI

It is delicate with immeasurable strength
So refined it cannot be measured
It is authority without domination
It is eloquent silence beyond compare
So true that it cannot be expressed

Many years ago, a baby girl was born to the emperor and empress of a far-away kingdom. As he looked at his newborn daughter the emperor thought to himself, "She is more precious to me than all of my wealth; even the sun, the moon, the stars, and all of the heavenly kingdoms." He named his daughter Shibumi.

To keep Shibumi safe, he built a beautiful garden with a high wall around it. Shibumi could play in the garden, but she was forbidden to go outside of its walls.

From the garden she could hear all of the sounds from the city beyond. She heard great sounds that boomed and small sounds that tinkled but she could not see what made them. She heard children laughing, and she thought, "Life must be wonderful outside the wall."

One day the children playing on the other side of the wall were making more noise than usual. The princess leaned against the wall, trying to hear what they were saying. To her surprise they were talking about her. "The emperor keeps his daughter in the walled garden because she's so ugly," said one child. "No," said another, "she's very fat and has long fangs and she only eats other children."

On hearing this the princess grew angry. A chestnut tree grew near the wall where she was standing. Though the princess had never climbed a tree before, she climbed quickly to the very top. "That's not true!" she called down to the children playing below. She was surprised to see that they were all ragged and dirty. From the sound of their laughter, she had imagined they were as beautiful and well-dressed as she.

On seeing the emperor's daughter, the children were terrified. "The emperor will send his troops to catch us," they cried to each other and ran away.

The city below looked far different to Shibumi than she had ever imagined. It was ugly and squalid, not grand and beautiful. In her jasmine-scented garden she had never noticed the smell from the garbage that was thrown into the streets for the dogs to eat. Beggars jangled bells as they pleaded for alms, and slave traders beat big drums as they dragged men and women in chains through the streets.

Shibumi had always thought that the city beyond her walled garden must be the most beautiful place on earth, but in reality only the palace and the little walled garden were beautiful.

Carefully she climbed down the chestnut tree. "I must ask my father why the city is so horrible," she thought. Then she realized that her father must never know that she climbed the chestnut tree and looked over the wall, for he would become very angry with her and probably have the poor tree cut down.

That night at dinner the emperor and empress noticed that Shibumi did not eat.

Of course her parents were worried, and sent for the physician. But he found nothing wrong. "Just see that she rests well," he said and left.

That night Shibumi lay in bed and wondered how her world and the one outside the wall could be so different. "I must find out more," she thought. As she gazed out her window she saw a great crane gliding high over the palace and thought, "That crane is just like a kite, he sits so still in the air." That gave her an idea, and she fell asleep.

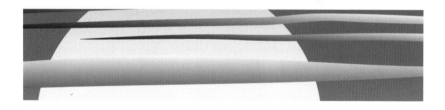

The next morning Shibumi asked her father if the royal kitemaker could make her a kite. "What a splendid idea," he thought, sure that a kite would cheer her up.

That afternoon the kitemaker came to the garden. He was old and wrinkled and had a twinkle in his eye, for he had made kites for years and he knew they were magic. "How may I serve her royal highness?" he asked.

"Please make me the biggest kite you can so I can see it no matter how high it flies," Shibumi replied.

"As you wish, your highness," the old man said, and left.

The next day he returned with the biggest kite he had ever made. With his help Shibumi flew it. "This one is not big enough," she said. "I need an even bigger kite."

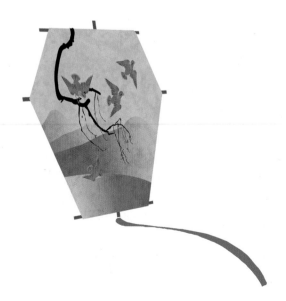

In a few days the kitemaker returned with a kite so large that everyone who saw it was in awe of his skill. Together, they flew the new kite. It was so big that a strong gust of wind almost lifted Shibumi off the ground. Nevertheless, she said to the kitemaker, "This kite is too small. Build me an even bigger one."

The kitemaker was astonished, "This kite almost pulled you off the ground. A bigger one may send you soaring in the air like a swallow."

"We shall see," said Shibumi. After a few weeks the old man came back with an even bigger kite. Everyone who saw it agreed that it was the most magnificent kite ever made.

The old kitemaker had made kites for many years and knew that kites, like Shibumi, could say much in their eloquent silence. He knelt down by the princess and said, "For a kite to be true, its purpose must be stated."

"I wish it would end the suffering in my father's city," said Shibumi.

"And how do you plan to do that?" asked the kitemaker with a smile.

"I cannot tell you," said Shibumi.

The kitemaker had seen the suffering in the city, for he had lived there all his life. He knew that only Shibumi could change it. "Remember this, princess. Whatever you ask of me, as long as it is part of what this kite must do, I will do it for you without question."

"Then," said the princess, "I must fly the kite from the highest tower of the castle, and my father will have you put to death because of it."

"I am old and it's time I became more like my creations. Let's go now, for there is a good wind."

The emperor was worried when he heard what his daughter was going to do, but when he saw how excited she was he didn't have the heart to say no. Besides, how would she ever be able to fly a kite from the highest tower?

Shibumi's parents watched from the garden as the kite was raised to the tower. Then they grew fearful when they saw someone holding on to the kite as it plunged toward the ground. Soon it caught an updraft and soared high overhead.

"Why, that old kitemaker is half crazy," said the emperor.

"But it's too small to be the kitemaker," said the empress.

"Oh, spirits of heavenly peace," they said together. "It's not the kitemaker, it's Shibumi." They called the guards and rushed to the tower. There they found the old kitemaker sitting on the edge of the tower wall holding the thin string that held Shibumi high in the air. "Bring her down this instant!" bellowed the emperor.

"If I begin to pull in the string before her wish is granted, she has told me that she will cut the string for the gods of the sky to claim her," said the kitemaker.

The emperor clenched his fists. "Are you disobeying me?" he cried.

"No, your highness, I am not. Your daughter ordered me to do this. She has a message for you."

"Well what is it, you fool?" shouted the emperor.

"She says she will not come down until the city below her is as beautiful as the palace, or the palace is as squalid as the city."

"That's impossible," stammered the emperor. "I shall have that kite taken from you," he added with a snarl.

"I will gladly give it to anyone you wish, but it is very tricky to handle and the slightest movement could cause it to crash to earth," said the kitemaker.

"Oh gods of the air," cried the emperor, "give him help to steady his hands."

"One more thing," said the kitemaker. "She says she loves you more than life, but the pain of the city is more than she can bear." The emperor stormed from the tower. He was mad with fear for his beloved daughter.

That evening the emperor called his councilors together. "Gather all the craftsmen together. Tonight we will rebuild the city."

After he left the room the councilors began to talk among themselves. "The emperor has lost his mind. You cannot change in one night what has taken years to become."

"He should be stopped," said the most powerful shogun. "I will settle this tonight before he wrecks us all."

At midnight, a lone archer crept up the tower stairs with bow and arrow ready. But the old kitemaker had seen such treachery before and was ready as well.

He knew the archer had come to kill him, causing the kite to spin wildly out of the sky and crash to the ground. The nobles were not about to give up any of their wealth — built upon the suffering of the inhabitants of that same city.

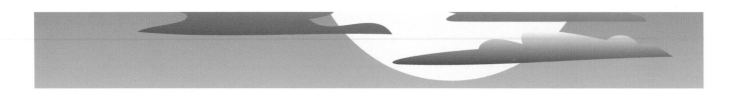

The kitemaker saw the archer raise his bow. "Hold tight, princess!" he called as he jumped from the tower. The gods of the sky took pity on them both and sent a strong wind. The perfection of the kite was such that the wind carried them high into the night clouds, where they disappeared from sight.

A servant who was watching told the emperor what had happened. The emperor was grief stricken. That night he arrested his councilors and threw them into prison. "I will do as my daughter wished. Let a thousand kites fly above the city in her memory."

That very night, in the depths of his grief, the emperor began to think. He began to consider why some people have so much and others so little.

The years passed and, indeed, a change did come to the city, and to the kingdom as well. The emperor kept his word and he worked day and night to do what was right and good for his people.

Now the city and the palace had been attacked by angry nobles whose greed was far greater than their compassion. The war was not going well for the emperor. "Am I doing all this for nothing?" he was often heard to say. "If only my daughter were here." The emperor was growing old and tired. As much as he tried to set things right, more wrongs appeared. It seemed as if there was more war in the kingdom now than ever before. Finally the emperor ordered the kites to be taken down.

It so happened that one of the street urchins who long ago had seen the princess shout at them from the garden wall grew to be a young man and a samurai in the personal service of the emperor.

One day the young samurai thought, "What if the princess did not perish that night, long ago? Perhaps the kite carried her far away and somehow, by the grace of the sky gods, she still lives." He asked the emperor for leave to attend to family matters. The emperor granted him his request.

The young samurai slipped through the siege line and headed for the open road disguised as a ronin, a samurai in the service of no lord. He traveled the country far and wide. After many months, on the northern tip of the kingdom he heard a strange story. The story told that years before, a spirit child had fallen from the sky and now was attended by a wrinkled old demon who let no one near her. They had vanished into the wilderness.

"Could this be the princess and the kitemaker?" thought the samurai. That night he set out for the wilderness. For weeks he braved cold and hunger along the windswept ocean coast. One day he saw a kite flying over the waves. As he drew closer he saw a small fishing shack. Next to it stood a beautiful young woman. It was she who flew the kite. But as he approached she ran behind some rocks and disappeared.

He did this for three days and nights, yet each time he approached, she ran away and hid. "I will have to reach her some other way," the samurai thought. He then built a beautiful kite, and in the morning he flew it above the fishing shack. Soon the girl appeared with her kite, but this time she walked right up to the samurai.

"Why are you here?" she asked. "Samurais are men of war; they do not fly kites."

"I am looking for a princess who flew from her home on a kite long ago," said the samurai.

"You are looking in the wrong place," said the girl.

"But if I were in the right place," said the samurai, "I would tell the princess that the emperor has tried with all his might to make the city as beautiful as the palace and now he is old and tired."

"I will go with you," said Shibumi. "But first I shall say goodbye to the kitemaker." She took the string of her kite and tied it to a little pile of neatly stacked stones that were the marker of the kitemaker's grave. "Goodbye old friend," she said. As they left the northern wilderness, they could see the kite waving high in the sky for miles.

After many months they reached the hills overlooking the city. The siege was still going on, and now, with the palace surrounded, it would be impossible for them to reach it. "I will have to return the way I left," said Shibumi. Within a week Shibumi had crafted a very large and beautiful kite. They placed it on the edge of a cliff, towering hundreds of feet in the air.

"I cannot be sure this will work," said Shibumi. "But there is no other way for me. Will you come with me?" The samurai agreed. Shibumi and the samurai took hold of the kite and jumped from the cliff. They fell a hundred feet straight down, but the kitemaker's art was perfect and Shibumi had learned all he had to teach. The first updraft caught them. Up into the sky they soared, far across the land below, and over the siege line to the palace in the center of the beautiful city at war.

The emperor was in the garden. Something in the sky caught his attention. He strained his weary eyes to see. His heart skipped a beat, for it was a kite, a very large kite not unlike the one which had carried his daughter away so many years before. Could it be possible? As quickly as he could, the emperor ran to the tallest tower as the kite flew low overhead. "Catch the rope, Father, and pull us down." His wildest dreams were answered. There must be compassionate gods in the heavenly kingdoms, for it was Shibumi. He caught the rope and pulled with all of his strength, but the kite was too strong. It took three other men to pull them down to the top of the tower.

Shibumi's first words to her father were the ones that he had hoped to hear through all those years. Now they freed him. "Yes, Father, the city is as beautiful as the palace."

The emperor was overjoyed, "Let ten thousand kites fly! My daughter has returned."

With new purpose and vigor the emperor's army rallied and broke the siege, putting the rebel nobles in retreat. But in the battle the emperor was mortally wounded. His daughter came to him as he lay on his death bed. "What you started so long ago by just flying a kite is so difficult to continue. Promise me that you will keep trying, in my place."

She smiled and said, "I will, Father."

That day one hundred thousand kites flew over the city. To this day they are flying. Both the city and the palace are still beautiful.

THE END

When I was thirteen my family moved to Hawaii. I left my home in Arkansas and two weeks later arrived in Honolulu. Things would never be the same. I left a racially segregated South (this was 1957) to live in a racial and cultural melting pot. My Southern accent dissolved into island pidgin English. Any racial bias that had been handed down to me vanished from pure necessity. I was one of three Haole (white) kids in my homeroom at Radford High. The rest of the kids were Hawaiian, Samoan, Japanese, Filipino, and every combination you could think of.

I became enthralled by the Japanese culture, mostly because it produced samurai movies. Samurai movies are to Japan what Westerns are to us. My hero was Toshiro Mifune and I saw every Kurosawa film made. Saturday afternoons were spent, if not at the beach, then at the Kaimuki movie theater in a wonderful afternoon of popcorn and gore.

All of my friends ate with chopsticks as well as forks. We had sushi snacks at school and in my neighborhood when somebody caught a tuna we had sashimi for everyone. We ate poi, lau lau, and dim sum—but it was the Japanese dishes I loved. The Japanese culture blended into the island life, and even dominated it. All of my family was affected. My mother, who was an artist, fell in love with Japanese rice paper and made beautiful floral collages out of it.

In 1985, I traveled to Japan on business. It was an interesting trip, but I left feeling disappointed. I had hoped to connect with what I thought would be the Japanese historical spirit. On the surface Japan looks like the West, but Westerners are rarely allowed to see into the Japanese heart. An old professor with whom I became friends in Kyoto acknowledges the barrier that exists in the Japanese psyche. As familiar as I have been with the Japanese culture, I never felt as though I could penetrate it, being a foreigner. But it holds romance and mystery for me. I respond strongly to Japanese art and history, and I am captivated by Zen writing.

I first heard the word Shibumi on that trip to Japan. I loved the way it sounded, but no one could translate it for me except to say it meant something fashionable or in good taste. Later on I gave it a meaning of my own, and out of that grew the story. As far as I know it has no basis in Japanese folk literature. Shibumi takes place in a culture that might have been, or in a place that exists even now—certainly in my heart.